The Mystery of the Goldfish Pond

THREE COUSINS DETECTIVE CLUB®

The Mystery of the Goldfish Pond

Elspeth Campbell Murphy
Illustrated by Joe Nordstrom

BETHANY HOUSE PUBLISHERS
MINNEAPOLIS, MINNESOTA 55438

The Mystery of the Goldfish Pond
Copyright © 1997
Elspeth Campbell Murphy

Cover and story illustrations by Joe Nordstrom

THREE COUSINS DETECTIVE CLUB® and TCDC® are
registered trademarks of Elspeth Campbell Murphy.

Scripture quotation is from the Bible in Today's English Version
(*Good News Bible*). Copyright © American Bible Society 1966,
1971, 1976, 1992

All rights reserved. No part of this publication may be reproduced,
stored in a retrieval system, or transmitted in any form or by any
means—electronic, mechanical, photocopying, recording, or
otherwise—without the prior written permission of the publisher
and copyright owners.

Published by Bethany House Publishers
A Ministry of Bethany Fellowship International
11400 Hampshire Avenue South
Minneapolis, Minnesota 55438
www.bethanyhouse.com

Printed in the United States of America by
Bethany Press International, Minneapolis, Minnesota 55438

Library of Congress Cataloging-in-Publication Data

Murphy, Elspeth Campbell.
    The mystery of the goldfish pond / by Elspeth Campbell
Murphy.
        p.   cm. — (Three Cousins Detective Club ; 15)
    Summary: While attending a fancy banquet, Timothy and his
cousins go out into the gardens and overhear a conversation that
draws them into an unexpected mystery.
    ISBN 1–55661–853–0
    [1. Cousins—Fiction.   2. Mystery and detective stories.]
I. Title. II. Series: Murphy, Elspeth Campbell. Three Cousins
Detective Club ; 15.
PZ7.M95316Mybj   1996
[Fic] — dc21   97–4645
                                                              CIP
                                                              AC

ELSPETH CAMPBELL MURPHY has been a familiar name in Christian publishing for over fifteen years, with more than seventy-five books to her credit and sales reaching five million worldwide. She is the author of the best-selling series *David and I Talk to God* and *The Kids From Apple Street Church*, as well as the 1990 Gold Medallion winner *Do You See Me, God?* A graduate of Trinity College and Moody Bible Institute, Elspeth and her husband, Mike, make their home in Chicago, where she writes full time.

Contents

No one who gossips can be trusted with a secret,
but you can put confidence in someone
who is trustworthy.

Proverbs 11:13

1

Dressing Up

*I*f there was anything worse than

- having to stop playing outside
- with your cousins
- in the late afternoon
- of a beautiful summer's day
- and come inside
- to take a bath
- and put on a suit and tie
- just so you could sing a solo
- at some dumb banquet,

then Timothy Dawson didn't know what it was.

The banquet was for grown-ups only, so Timothy would have been the only kid there. Except that his cousins Sarah-Jane Cooper and Titus McKay were coming along for moral support.

Titus and Sarah-Jane had to get dressed up, too, of course. But it wasn't so bad for them. They didn't have to *do* anything.

Timothy could tell that Sarah-Jane was actually very excited about getting dressed up and having her Aunt Sarah do her hair. But for Timothy's sake, Sarah-Jane was trying not to show it too much.

Titus wasn't exactly excited, but he felt OK about everything. Still, he acted grumpy, too. Timothy knew he was only doing that to be nice so that he—Timothy—wouldn't be the only grumpy one.

After they were dressed, Timothy's mother sat them around the kitchen table. They would have crackers and juice "to hold them" since they'd be eating dinner later than usual. But before they could even take a bite, Timothy's mother covered them up with three of his dad's old shirts. With the shirts on backwards, they looked like three kindergartners getting ready to finger-paint.

Timothy's sister, Priscilla, sat in her high chair and ate her little baby supper. She had

had a bath, too. But now she was in her jammies. And she knew something was up.

She narrowed her eyes and looked at her
brother and cousins suspiciously. One by one.

"Timmy go bye-bye?"

"Yes."

"Say-wah Zane go bye-bye?"

"Yes."

"Tidus go bye-bye?"

"Yes."

"Sibby *NO* go bye-bye?"

"Uh—well," said Timothy, bracing himself
for the howls.

But at that moment Priscilla's favorite baby-sitter arrived, making a big fuss over her as usual. Priscilla seemed to forget she even had a brother or cousins.

The sitter kept Priscilla so busy upstairs that they were all able to slip out without a war.

As the car pulled away, Timothy looked back at the house. He thought of Priscilla, all cozy in her jammies playing ring-around-a-rosy.

Some people had it so easy.

2

Going Out

*T*imothy's mother turned around from the front seat and smiled brightly at them. "You kids clean up real cute," she said.

Sarah-Jane laughed delightedly.

Titus rolled his eyes—but he did it with a cheerful grin.

Timothy, though, stayed serious. He was wondering about something. He was wondering: If he belched really, really loud, would his father stop and turn the car around?

That had actually happened once. Of course, *then* they had been on their way to a carnival—a place Timothy had really wanted to go to. He had been warned twice about the belching. The third time, his father had stopped and turned the car around.

They had gotten to the carnival eventually. But they had lost valuable time. And Timothy hadn't gotten to go on all the rides he had wanted to.

He had never belched in the car again.

If he tried it now, would his father stop and turn the car around?

Probably not.

Timothy knew his parents would guess that he was only trying to get out of this banquet thing. The words "best behavior" had been spoken by his parents more than eighty million times today already. So belching now would probably just get him grounded for the rest of his life.

Since Timothy was clearly not in the mood for conversation, his cousins turned to the grown-ups.

Titus said, "Uncle Paul, tell me again where it is we're going?"

"It's a retirement dinner for my boss," replied Timothy's father.

Titus thought about that for a minute. "And tell me again why *we're* going?"

His uncle laughed. "My boss's wife, Mrs. Pomeroy, once went to a concert where

Timothy's choir was singing songs from old Broadway musicals. Timothy had a solo, and it happened to be Mrs. Pomeroy's favorite song. So Mrs. Pomeroy decided Timothy should sing it at her husband's retirement dinner. And when Mrs. Pomeroy makes up her mind about something, look out!"

"Not only that," added Timothy's mother. "Mrs. Pomeroy is under the impression that Timothy is a perfect little angel."

This was greeted by hoots and snorts from his loyal cousins.

"WHY?" cried Titus and Sarah-Jane together.

"Beats me," said Timothy's mother. "Maybe it's because he looks and sounds like an angel when he's singing."

Timothy's father said seriously, "I hope everything goes well tonight. My boss was pretty upset this afternoon."

"Why?" asked Timothy's mother.

"He had written this memo outlining our plans for a new product. Top secret. If other companies found out our plans and beat us to it, it could cost us a bundle."

"And the memo is missing?" asked Timothy's mother in alarm.

"No, it turned out he had just misplaced it," said her husband. "But it was upsetting all the same." He said to the cousins, "So let's not do anything to shock Mr. and Mrs. Pomeroy. Best behavior, OK?"

"Absolutely," said Sarah-Jane.

"We promise not to embarrass you," said Titus.

"Whatever," said Timothy.

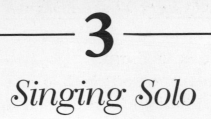

Singing Solo

"*S*o what are you going to sing tonight?" Titus asked as they followed Timothy's parents across the parking lot.

Timothy said, " 'I'm Just Wild About Harry.' "

His cousins stared at him. They were completely confused by this strange answer to a simple question.

"Who's Harry?" asked Sarah-Jane.

"And why are you wild about him?" asked Titus.

Nervous as he was, Timothy burst out laughing. "No! That's the name of the song!"

Sarah-Jane still looked confused. " 'I'm Just Wild About Harry' is the name of a *song*?"

"Yup," said Timothy. "It's Mrs. Pomeroy's favorite song."

Titus said, "How could that be *anybody's* favorite song?"

Timothy shrugged. "I don't know. If you're married to some guy named Harry, I guess. That's Mr. Pomeroy's first name.

"The plan is that the MC—the Master of Ceremonies—will get everyone to sit at their tables. And then—when Mr. and Mrs. Pomeroy come in to sit at the head table—that's when I sing 'I'm Just Wild About Harry.' Mr. Pomeroy doesn't know anything about it. It's a surprise."

"Oh," said Sarah-Jane. "Well, that will be nice." Timothy agreed with what Sarah-Jane seemed to be thinking. As surprises went, it wasn't exactly earthshaking.

"At least you'll get your solo over with early," said Titus.

"Yes," agreed Timothy. "There is that. After the song, we'll eat. And then there will be speeches. Boring, boring, boring speeches."

But, Timothy thought to himself, being bored was better than being nervous any day.

If he could just get through his solo, he could live with being bored.

The piano player was Timothy's choir director, so that helped a lot. They had already rehearsed together. And, as soon as he started singing, Timothy got over his nervousness. He sang with real gusto.

Mr. Pomeroy was absolutely delighted with his surprise.

After Timothy had sung the song through, everyone joined in, laughing and clapping along.

There was a lot of applause for Mr. and Mrs. Pomeroy. And there was a lot of applause for Timothy and his teacher, too.

Timothy made his way to his parents' table. Everyone was telling him what a great job he had done. There was nothing like facing something scary, coming through it, and being on the other side—having it behind you instead of in front of you. And doing a good job on something hard? What could be better than that?

Timothy saw that his parents' table was full

of grown-ups. He and Titus and Sarah-Jane would get a table all to themselves. Not too shabby. They even got to order from the children's menu so that they wouldn't have to have something ghastly for dinner.

Sarah-Jane wanted macaroni and cheese. Titus wanted franks and beans. And Timothy wanted chicken fingers. Actually, they all wanted a little bit of everything. So their waiter said he would have them divide it up in the kitchen so that each plate would have some of each. They also got Jell-O and carrot sticks and olives. Timothy loved black olives. He loved to put one on each finger and when he had his hand all filled up, eat the olives one by one. But he was supposed to be on his best behavior—so maybe not tonight. . . .

The evening was off to a good start. Even though it would get pretty boring pretty fast, Timothy felt great to be alive.

What could possibly go wrong?

4

Behaving Beautifully

Whe they were waiting for their food, Timothy, Titus, and Sarah-Jane sat quietly and looked around the banquet hall.

They were seated at a small table by the side of the room, a little ways apart from the grown-ups.

Anyone seeing them would just think they were three beautifully behaved kids doing nothing.

But actually, they were casing the joint.

They had picked up the expression from an old movie they had seen on TV. It was something crooks said when they were looking for a way to rob a place.

The cousins had no intention of stealing anything, of course. They were detectives, not crooks. But—as detectives—they liked to notice what was going on around them. Not that there was likely to be anything mysterious going on. Still—you never knew. Even in the most boring place it was good to stay alert.

And the place wasn't even all that boring.

The dinner was being held in a very popular restaurant called The Pavilion. Actually, the restaurant was more like a group of separate banquet rooms that people could rent for parties. That way, different dinners could be going on all at the same time. The Pavilion was famous for its gardens.

Titus and Sarah-Jane had never been to The Pavilion before.

Timothy had been there once when he was little. He had been the ring bearer at a wedding, and the reception had been held at The Pavilion. But that had been in the day-time.

It suddenly occurred to Timothy that he wasn't out after dark very often. And that was too bad, because he was an outdoors kind of person. But now, when he got to be out late, he was still stuck inside.

Timothy sighed and looked around the room some more.

A cheerful voice behind him said, "Looking for a way out?"

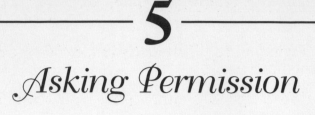

5

Asking Permission

*T*imothy jumped.

Out of the corner of his eye, he had seen their waiter, Bob, coming back with their food. So it wasn't as if he hadn't been alert or anything. It's just that it's always a little startling when someone seems to read your mind.

"How did you know what I was thinking?" Timothy asked him.

Bob laughed. "Believe me. I've served at enough of these dinners to know how boring they can be if you don't really know what's going on. Or even if you do."

"So—*is* there a way out?" asked Sarah-Jane wistfully. She sounded as if she were almost afraid to hope.

Titus said, "Tell us, please! We beg of you!"

Bob laughed again. "OK. You seem like nice kids. I wouldn't be telling you this if I thought you were going to run around screaming or anything."

"Never!" cried Timothy as if he couldn't imagine anyone ever doing such a thing.

"OK, here's the deal," said Bob. He looked both ways as if he were afraid of being overheard. Then he leaned forward and talked out of the corner of his mouth.

The cousins knew he was just kidding. But it was fun to play along.

"You see those floor-to-ceiling curtains right behind you?" asked Bob.

The cousins looked without being at all obvious about it. They nodded.

"Good," said Bob. "Now behind those curtains is a glass wall. Only it's not a wall. It's a sliding door."

"Freedom!" gasped Timothy.

"So near and yet so far," sighed Titus.

"What's out there?" asked Sarah-Jane.

"The garden," replied Bob. "I'll open the door a little way so that you can slip in and out without having to go all the way to the front door by the speakers' table. But ask your parents first," he added as he left them.

Timothy looked over toward his parents' table. His father was in deep conversation with some guy from work. Timothy thought both men looked worried, and he had a hunch something was wrong. But Timothy knew it was sometimes hard for him to tell whether he really had a hunch or whether he was just longing for something—anything—interesting to happen.

The cousins talked it over as they ate and decided that just Timothy should be the one to do the talking. Three kids rushing over there all talking at once was a surefire way *not* to be allowed outside.

Between dinner and dessert the cousins went over to the grown-ups' table. Their timing was bad in that Mrs. Pomeroy was coming over to chat at just the same time.

"Here are your three little angels!" she exclaimed to Timothy's mother.

Before Timothy's mother could gulp out a reply, Mrs. Pomeroy turned to the cousins. "Have you had a nice summer, my dears? What have you been doing?"

"Um—" said Timothy. They had done plenty, but now his mind was a complete blank. It was always that way when someone said, "What's new?" He could never think of a thing. "Um—" said Timothy again. "Well, there's the T.C.D.C."

"Indeed!" beamed Mrs. Pomeroy. "And what's a 'teesy-deesy'?"

"It's letters," explained Timothy. "Capital T. Capital C. Capital D. Capital C. It stands for the Three Cousins Detective Club."

"Ah," said Mrs. Pomeroy more to herself than to the cousins. "Now that *is* interesting." She sounded as if she really thought it was.

And Timothy found *that* interesting. But he didn't have time to wonder about it. The waiters were bringing out dessert. And Timothy wanted to get permission to go outside before his ice cream melted.

His father looked pretty doubtful about letting them go. But help came from an unexpected source.

Mrs. Pomeroy.

6

Getting Away

"Now, Paul," boomed Mrs. Pomeroy. "You know that I am the last person in the world to interfere! But I think you should let the children walk in the gardens. They are such *lovely* children! What trouble could they possibly get into?"

Timothy's parents looked at each other as if to say, "How much time do we have to answer that?"

But they gave their permission—along with some rules:

"Stay together and don't wander off."

The cousins nodded. That was always the rule when they were in a strange place.

"Don't run around screaming."

Again the cousins nodded. Bob the waiter

had already covered that one.

"Don't get your good clothes dirty."

That one was a little harder to control. But if you weren't allowed to run around, it didn't seem that you would get all that grubby.

"Sounds do-able, Uncle Paul," said Titus. Sarah-Jane agreed.

"OK," said Timothy to his parents. "We'll see you guys later."

Before they could answer, Mrs. Pomeroy said, "Take your time, my dears. And then you must come back and tell me all about it."

After dessert, people had been milling around, taking a break between dinner and the speakers. But now the MC stepped up to the microphone and asked for everyone's attention. The cousins took that as their cue to leave.

Being detectives, they were used to moving around stealthily when they needed to so that they wouldn't be seen or heard.

"Well," said Titus as they slipped quietly out into the night. "Getting away was easier than I thought it would be."

"Too easy?" replied Timothy.

"What do you mean?" asked Sarah-Jane.

"I'm not sure," said Timothy thoughtfully. "But didn't you notice how Mrs. Pomeroy practically threw us out of there? What was that all about?"

"Maybe she was afraid we would start a food fight," said Titus. He wasn't serious.

"We're too darling for that," said Sarah-Jane. She wasn't serious, either. "But when you think about it, she did kind of *insist*. How could Aunt Sarah and Uncle Paul say 'no' after that?"

"Yes," said Titus. "And what did she mean about coming back and telling her all about it? Tell her what? That we saw some plants?"

"Something odd is going on," said Timothy. "I just know it."

7

Exploring the Jungle

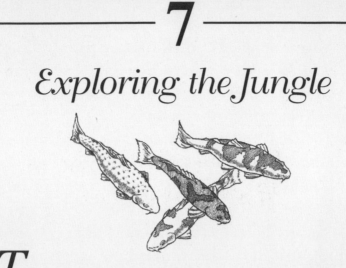

The cousins had been so busy wondering about Mrs. Pomeroy that they hadn't noticed the gardens at first.

"Wow!" said Titus. "It's a jungle out here!"

It wasn't really, of course. But the gardens had been carefully planted to look wild.

Seeing it at night, with colored lights strung all around, made it look even more magical. It was as if an everyday kind of place was wearing a disguise to make it look like an enchanted garden out of a fairy tale.

It was very exciting to be out in that garden. Alone. At night. There were other people around. But the cousins weren't *with* anyone except themselves. It was enough to make them want to run every which way, trying to take it all in. But they didn't.

Fascinating little stone paths led off in all directions.

Titus wanted to go to the left.

Sarah-Jane wanted to go to the right.

Timothy wanted to go straight ahead.

But they had been told to stay together.

So—since Timothy was the reason they were at The Pavilion in the first place—his cousins let him choose.

From somewhere up ahead there came a gentle sound of splashing water.

Timothy headed in that direction with his cousins following along. The path wasn't all that narrow. But they walked in single file anyway. It made them feel more like explorers.

Suddenly the path turned, and the cousins found themselves at the edge of a beautiful pond.

As an explorer, Timothy wanted to name it after himself. But his cousins wouldn't go along with it. It was one thing to let him lead. But they drew the line at Lake Timothy. They finally agreed on Cousins' Pond.

It really was a beautiful spot. There was a fountain in the middle of the pond and clusters of water lilies here and there.

But what really caught their attention was something moving. Lots of things moving.

"Ooo! Look!" said Sarah-Jane. "Fish!"

Timothy, who loved art, gasped when he saw all the gorgeous designs and colors. Big fish. Little fish. They were the most beautiful fish he had ever seen.

Titus, who loved science, was puzzled. "What kind of fish are those?" he asked. "I

think the little ones are goldfish. I know goldfish can get pretty big. But not as big as those. So what kind are they?"

Sarah-Jane, who loved all kinds of stories, especially folktales, said, "Maybe they're magical fish. And they will grant us three wishes."

"Good," said Titus. "Then I wish they'd tell us what kind of fish they are."

There's something hypnotic about watching fish. They're so graceful and peaceful that you hardly want to do anything else.

Timothy felt torn. He didn't want to stop something so good as watching the fish. But he didn't want to miss doing other good stuff, either.

In the end, he and his cousins decided to keep exploring the rest of the gardens. The goldfish pond would still be there, and they could always find their way back.

8

Hiding

The cousins were in for another surprise.

The path ran alongside a little stream. As they followed it, they noticed the sound of the water becoming louder.

They soon saw why.

They turned a bend and saw that the splash came from a little waterfall. A clear sheet of water fell out and over from a rock ledge above them. Behind the waterfall, the rock wall curved to form a kind of shallow, cozy cave.

"Do you think we could go back there?" asked Timothy. "I think I see a way to step around behind the waterfall without getting wet."

"Sure," said Sarah-Jane. "I don't see why

not. I mean, there are no signs that say you can't go back there."

"That's probably because nobody thought of it," said Titus. "But there's no way we could wreck anything. And as long as we're quiet. . . ."

Timothy tried naming the place Timothy Falls. But his cousins would have none of it. So they agreed on Explorer Falls.

Then the three explorer-cousins stepped carefully between the rock wall and the falling water. There was enough room for the three of them in the little cave. But grown-ups wouldn't have fit. That was OK. Probably no grown-ups would have gotten the idea to go back there in the first place.

"This is so cool!" breathed Sarah-Jane.

"EX-cellent!" agreed Titus.

"Neat-O!" said Timothy.

Looking out through the water made the plants and flowers run together in a blur of pretty colors. Timothy wondered if a good painter could copy the way it looked and get it just right. He wished he could.

Timothy felt very pleased. It wasn't his wa-terfall, of course. (It wasn't even named after him.) But he felt responsible for the fun they were having, since it had been his idea to go back there.

But on the other hand—now that he stopped to think about it—Timothy wasn't so sure that going behind the waterfall could be called being on their absolutely best behavior. . . .

He knew that Titus and Sarah-Jane wouldn't try to put the blame on him if they got in trouble. But still, Timothy felt responsible, because it had been his idea. Besides, they had the rest of the garden to explore. And they had all wanted to go back to the goldfish pond.

Timothy figured it was time to move on. He motioned to his cousins.

They were just about to slip out the way they had come when they heard voices.

And some detective instinct warned them to be very, very quiet.

9

Overhearing

Up till now, Timothy, Titus, and Sarah-Jane had just been playing. But suddenly they realized they were in the middle of something more serious.

There was something about the way the voices sounded. Quiet. But edgy and tense.

The cousins knew that listening in on other people's conversations was called eavesdropping. And they knew it wasn't a very nice thing to do. But in this case they were pretty much stuck.

The speakers—two men—sounded as if they didn't want to be overheard. But the voices had started up before the cousins could come out. And if they came out now, the men would *know* they had been overheard. It would be awkward—to say the least!

Even with the splashing of the waterfall, they couldn't help overhearing what the men were saying. Most of it. Some of the words were kind of hard to understand.

"Did you get it?" asked the first man.

"No, it's not there yet."

"What's the —blem?"

"No prob—It will be there."

"Where?"

"By the —oy."

"Too —isky?"

"No. —idden. —ake —urtle."

"He'd better not —ess this up! Or he doesn't get a —ime!"

"—e knows —at."

"Check —ack."

"Yes. —oon."

The cousins couldn't see the men. But they heard footsteps going off in opposite directions.

They waited in silence for a few moments just to be sure.

From far away they could hear groups of people talking and laughing.

But there were no tense, quiet voices nearby.

Slowly, carefully, Timothy leaned around the edge of their little cave and peeked out.

"All clear," he whispered to his cousins. "Come on. Now's our chance."

10

Talking Things Over

"*W*hew!" said Titus softly when they were safely back on the path. "What was *that* all about?"

Sarah-Jane said, "Something's going on. That's for sure. But what?"

"Well, let's think about it," said Timothy.

This was something the cousins did all the time. Talking things over. Thinking things through.

As they talked, they continued to follow the stone path through the garden. They kept their voices low. (They didn't want to be overheard, either!)

"OK," said Titus. "Some*body* was supposed to leave some*thing* for these guys. But it wasn't there yet. And the first guy was nervous about that. But the second guy said it was no problem. He said the thing would be there and that he would—what? Check back soon? I think that's what he said."

Timothy and Sarah-Jane agreed that it was.

"It all sounded so sneaky, didn't it?" said Sarah-Jane. "I mean, the way they were meeting in the garden and whispering like that. And the first guy said it would be 'isky.' Risky? And the second guy said that the thing would be 'idden.' Hidden? And the guy who was supposed to bring this thing—whatever it is—wouldn't get paid if he messed up. Wouldn't get a 'ime.' Dime?"

"I think we got the gist of it," said Timothy. "And we know this thing—whatever it is—is going to be hidden by the 'oy.' "

" 'Oy,' " said Sarah-Jane. "What's an 'oy'?"

"We couldn't hear the beginning of the word," said Timothy. "But we figured out the other ones."

The cousins were quiet for a moment, silently running through the alphabet.

"Boy!" said Titus.

"I'll say!" agreed Timothy. "This one is much harder."

"No," said Titus. "I wasn't saying, 'Boy, this is hard.' I meant 'boy' as in 'oy.' 'It will be there by the *boy*.' But that doesn't make sense, does it? Wouldn't you leave something *with* the boy? Or give it *to* the boy?"

Sarah-Jane said, "Boys don't stand still long enough for you to leave anything *by* them. How about a person's name? You know, like Mrs. *Pomeroy*."

"*Pomeroy* ends right," said Timothy. "But I don't think the word the guy used was as long as that."

"How about just *Roy*, then?" suggested Sarah-Jane. "That could be a man's name. Or *Joy* if it was a woman."

"It still doesn't sound right," said Titus. "You don't put *the* in front of a name. 'It will be there by *the Roy*.' 'It will be there by *the Joy*.' It doesn't sound right."

Sarah-Jane and Timothy agreed that it didn't make sense.

"*Toy*," said Timothy. " 'It will be there by the *toy*.' But you wouldn't have toys in a place like this, would you? And what was all that

44

about 'ake' and 'urtle'?"

His cousins shook their heads.

Sometimes you could figure things out by talking it over.

And sometimes you couldn't.

11

Taking a Rest

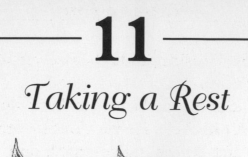

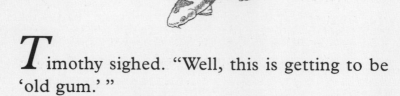

*T*imothy sighed. "Well, this is getting to be 'old gum.' "

He knew that Titus and Sarah-Jane would understand exactly what he meant. It was an expression they had made up for when they had talked about something too long without getting anywhere. It felt the same as when you've chewed a piece of gum for too long. Tedious. And you just want to stop and start over with something fresh.

The cousins knew they could drive themselves crazy trying to figure something out when they didn't have all the facts. When they felt themselves talking—or even thinking—in circles, it was good to take a rest.

So the cousins made themselves stop talking in circles.

But they found they had been *walking* in circles. A big circle, anyway. Because they were almost back by the big goldfish pond.

Suddenly, Timothy—who was still leading—stopped dead in his tracks. Titus and Sarah-Jane stumbled into him.

"Listen!" said Timothy softly. "Did you hear that?"

"Hear what?" asked Sarah-Jane.

"I don't hear anything unusual," said Titus.

"That's funny. . . ." murmured Timothy, more to himself than to his cousins.

"Funny ha-ha? Or funny weird?" asked Titus.

"Funny weird," said Timothy.

"What's funny weird?" asked Sarah-Jane.

Timothy said, "I could have sworn I heard somebody humming just now. You know how people will have a song going around in their head? And they don't even realize that they're humming it out loud? It sounded like that. A man humming."

Titus looked at him with a puzzled frown.

"What's so weird about a guy humming, Tim?" he asked.

"It's *what* he was humming," said Timothy.

"And that was. . . ?" asked Sarah-Jane.

" 'I'm Just Wild About Harry,' " said Timothy.

12

Humming a Catchy Tune

"*A*re you sure, Tim?" asked Sarah-Jane. "You just said that a person can have a song going around in his head. Maybe that's happening to you. Maybe you're still hearing that song inside your head because you practiced it so much. I didn't hear anything. And neither did Ti."

But Timothy just shook his head. "No, I heard it, all right. I'm sure of it."

Titus and Sarah-Jane didn't argue. They knew that Timothy had a good eye for art and a good ear for music.

Titus said, " 'I'm Just Wild About Harry' has a really catchy tune. It's not surprising that someone would hum it if he'd just heard it."

"My point exactly," said Timothy. "Where would someone have heard that song recently?"

"At the retirement dinner, of course," began Sarah-Jane. Then she stopped. "Oh! I see what you're getting at. All the people who heard that song should be inside listening to speeches right now. Not out wandering around in the garden. But maybe someone slipped away to go to the bathroom or something. And then maybe he decided to come outside for some fresh air."

"It could happen," said Titus. "Or how about this? Maybe the guy you heard humming doesn't have anything to do with the retirement dinner at all. Maybe 'I'm Just Wild About Harry' just happens to be his favorite song."

Timothy grinned at him. "You said it yourself. How could 'I'm Just Wild About Harry' be *anybody's* favorite song? It's probably nothing. It just struck me as odd, that's all."

They stood still and listened hard. But they didn't hear anyone humming—just the splash of water in the goldfish pond.

"Oh, wow, thanks so much, Tim," said Titus. He sounded disgusted—but in a kidding way.

"What did *I* do?" exclaimed Timothy.

"You brought up that song!" wailed Titus. "Now I've got it going around and around in *my* head. I'll never get rid of it!"

"Sure you will," said Timothy. "Just try humming 'The Twelve Days of Christmas' or something."

"Hey, it worked!" cried Titus after a moment. "But—now I can't get 'The Twelve Days of Christmas' out of my head!"

Timothy shrugged. "I just told you how to get rid of 'I'm Just Wild About Harry,' " said Timothy. "I can't do everything, you know."

Sarah-Jane patted Titus's shoulder. "There, there," she said like a kindly old teacher. "You just need something else to drive you crazy so you'll forget about all those songs. Now, why don't you come over and look at the fish? What is it they're called again?"

Titus snarled at his cousins. "You two are warped, you know that?"

13

Finding Out

T imothy, Titus, and Sarah-Jane went to the edge of the pond (Cousins' Pond) to get a better look at the fish. It was then that they saw something they hadn't even noticed before: A bridge. The pond was kind of long and narrow, and the bridge was at the other end.

The cousins forced themselves to walk calmly along the path to the foot of the bridge. There was something about a bridge that made you just want to *run* to the middle and look down.

But the cousins knew that there was nothing that made grown-ups more nervous than kids running—especially in a fancy place. The last thing they wanted was to get stopped by somebody and sent back to the dinner.

So they forced themselves to *walk* to the middle of the bridge.

The view of the goldfish pond was even better from up there.

There were lights built into the edge of the pond all the way around. As the fish swam past, the light reflected off their shiny scales. It looked as if they were made of gold and silver and precious jewels.

From up on the little bridge Sarah-Jane spotted something else. "Ooo! Look!" she said, pointing to the edge of the pond. "A turtle! It's sitting so still!" She stopped and thought about this. "Is it real? It looks like a decoration I saw in a catalog once."

The boys looked where she was pointing. The turtle was almost hidden by some plants at the edge of the pond. And it was almost the same color as the rock it was sitting on.

"Turtles can sit still for a long time," said Titus. "But it looks like a decoration to me. It's hard to tell."

"No," said Timothy. "It must be real. I remember looking at those plants when we came by the pond the first time. I remember thinking I had never seen flowers like that before. The

turtle wasn't on the rock then. I would have
noticed it for sure. So he must have just
climbed up on the rock. And if he can climb,
he must be real."

"Must be," said Titus.

Just then a couple about their grand-
parents' age came over the bridge. They
smiled at the cousins. And the cousins could
almost hear them thinking: What beautifully
behaved children!

The lady said to them, "The fish are lovely,

aren't they? They were especially bred to have beautiful designs on their backs. That's because they're pond fish. In an aquarium you see fish from the side. In a pond, you see fish from above."

Her husband interrupted her. "Can you tell she's a teacher?"

Everyone laughed. But then Titus said, "Finally! Someone who can tell me what kind of fish these are!"

The lady beamed at him. There's nothing teachers like more than kids who really want to know stuff.

"Well, the little ones are goldfish, of course," she said. "And the big ones are from Japan. They're called *koi*."

14

Taking a Look

*T*he nice couple went on across the bridge. But the cousins stayed right where they were. They stood staring at one another as if they were all thinking the same thing but couldn't get the words out.

Finally Timothy said excitedly (but quietly), "By the 'oy.' By the *koi*?! Is that what those two guys were talking about? That something is hidden by the pond?"

"I think that's *exactly* right," said Titus. "But *where*? The pond is a big place. With lots of hiding places."

Out of the blue Sarah-Jane said thoughtfully, "That turtle hasn't budged an inch."

The boys stared at her.

"S-J!" said Timothy. "Please try to keep

56

up! We stopped talking about that turtle a long time ago. What does it matter if he's real or not?"

Sarah-Jane said, "You two are always teasing me because I like to look at catalogs."

This time Timothy and Titus turned to stare at each other. They had completely lost the thread of the conversation.

Sarah-Jane sighed impatiently. "Will you two please try to keep up? I saw a turtle just like that one in a catalog once. And sure—you put it in your yard for decoration. But it's not *just* for decoration. The turtle is hollow inside. You can hide an extra key in there in case you lock yourself out of the house."

"It's hollow," repeated Titus. "It's a fake turtle. And it's hollow inside."

" '-ake urtle-' " said Timothy.

This time they couldn't stop themselves from running. They rushed down the bridge and around the pond until they were right in front of the turtle.

Then they just stood and looked at it.

They were *dying* of curiosity. But they weren't sure what to do next.

Timothy said, "The guy must have put the

turtle here while we were gone, walking around the garden. That's why I didn't see it there before."

"And the waterfall guys haven't gotten it yet," said Titus. "But they could be here any minute."

Sarah-Jane said, "I know this is none of our business. But let's just take a quick look inside. I mean, what if it's filled with stolen diamonds or something? We'd have to call the police."

Timothy and Titus agreed with her.

Timothy carefully stepped over a couple of rocks, scooped up the turtle, and tucked it inside his suit coat. For the first time in his life he was glad to be wearing a suit.

Then the three detective cousins slipped quietly over to a bench that was partly hidden by some bushes.

Timothy's hands were shaking from excitement. But he managed to open the turtle.

15

Helping Out

Maybe—because they were thinking of diamonds—they were disappointed to see only a folded-up paper inside.

Timothy pulled it out and opened it up.

"Oh, it's just some kind of business memo," said Sarah-Jane.

"It's none of our business," said Titus.

But Timothy said, "No! No, it *is* our business. Or at least my dad's business."

Titus and Sarah-Jane looked at him in surprise.

Timothy pointed to a little design at the top of the page. "See that design? It's called a *logo*. Just about every company has one. It's like a little picture that stands for the company. And *this* logo is the one for my dad's company."

The cousins tried to read the memo. They were all good readers, but they couldn't make head or tail of it. But they could read the name of the person who wrote it: Mr. Harry Pomeroy.

Titus said, "Could this be what Uncle Paul was talking about on the way over here? This is a photocopy. Do you suppose—I mean, maybe someone took the secret memo and made a copy of it. And put the original back, so that no one would know. Except, it got put back in the wrong place."

Sarah-Jane said, "You mean someone from Uncle Paul's company was going to sell the

company's secrets to another company? Is that what's going on here?"

Timothy said, "Maybe the guy who left the turtle is the guy I heard humming a while ago. And what about the waterfall guys? If they come back and the turtle isn't there, they'll think he hasn't brought it yet. Let's go."

They made a beeline back to the dinner.

The cousins slipped in through the sliding door. The speeches were over, and people were standing around talking.

Timothy was able to get his parents' attention. They must have seen something was up, because they came over right away.

So did Mr. and Mrs. Pomeroy.

It took a while—quite a while—to explain what all had happened.

Mr. Pomeroy heaved a sigh of relief. "When I couldn't find the memo, I was afraid someone might have made a copy of it. You kids kept the information from falling into the wrong hands! Isn't it amazing how it all worked out?"

Mrs. Pomeroy said, "I just love The Pavilion, don't you? Unfortunately, it's the ideal place to pass something along. You have the gardens. And all these different banquets going on at the same time. Oh, yes. If information were going to be passed, this would be the place to do it."

Timothy said suddenly, "*That's* why you talked my parents into letting us go out! You hoped we'd see something odd and come back and tell you about it!"

"You're right, of course," said Mrs. Pomeroy. "And you have done more than I could ever have hoped for! I had a feeling someone might try something tonight. But I couldn't leave the dinner. You children could. So I sent Bob the waiter to suggest it to you. And when I heard that you were detectives! Well, that settled it. But I couldn't tell you what I wanted you to do in case the wrong person overheard. And to think that Harry says I read too many mysteries! Ha!"

"I won't say that ever again!" said Mr. Pomeroy.

Timothy's father and Mr. Pomeroy had a good idea of who was behind the whole thing. And Timothy was glad to let them take over.

But there was just one more thing.

"Dad, do you think I could keep the turtle?" he asked. "It's not for me. It's for Priscilla. I thought it would be nice to bring something home for her. Poor kid. She doesn't get out much."

The End

Series for Young Readers*
From Bethany House Publishers

THE ADVENTURES OF CALLIE ANN
by Shannon Mason Leppard

Readers will giggle their way through the true-to-life escapades of Callie Ann Davies and her many North Carolina friends.

ASTROKIDS™
by Robert Elmer

Space scooters? Floating robots? Jupiter ice cream? Blast into the future for out-of-this-world, zero-gravity fun with the AstroKids on space station *CLEO-7.*

BACKPACK MYSTERIES
by Mary Carpenter Reid

This excitement-filled mystery series follows the mishaps and adventures of Steff and Paulie Larson as they strive to help often-eccentric relatives crack their toughest cases.

THE CUL-DE-SAC KIDS
by Beverly Lewis

Each story in this lighthearted series features the hilarious antics and predicaments of nine endearing boys and girls who live on Blossom Hill Lane.

JANETTE OKE'S ANIMAL FRIENDS
by Janette Oke

Endearing creatures from the farm, forest, and zoo discover their place in God's world through various struggles, mishaps, and adventures.

RUBY SLIPPERS SCHOOL
by Stacy Towle Morgan

Join the fun as home-schoolers Hope and Annie Brown visit fascinating countries and meet inspiring Christians from around the world!

THREE COUSINS DETECTIVE CLUB®
by Elspeth Campbell Murphy

Famous detective cousins Timothy, Titus, and Sarah-Jane learn compelling Scripture-based truths while finding—and solving—intriguing mysteries.

*(ages 7–10)